W9-CFG-482

HORSES
with
WINGS

by DENNIS HASELEY

paintings *by* LYNN CURLEE

A Laura Geringer Book
An Imprint of HarperCollins*Publishers*

HORSES *with* WINGS

Text copyright © 1993 by Dennis Haseley

Illustrations copyright © 1993 by Lynn Curlee

Printed in the U.S.A.   All rights reserved.

Designed by David Saylor

1 2 3 4 5 6 7 8 9 10

❖

First Edition

Library of Congress Cataloging-in-Publication Data

Haseley, Dennis.

  Horses with wings / by Dennis Haseley ; paintings by Lynn Curlee.

    p.   cm.

  "A Laura Geringer book."

  Summary: During the Franco-Prussian War, Léon Gambetta
escapes from Paris in a balloon and organizes an army in the French
countryside to fight against the Prussian invaders.

  ISBN 0-06-022885-7. — ISBN 0-06-022886-5 (lib. bdg.)

  1. Gambetta, Léon, 1838–1882—Juvenile fiction.

2. Franco–Prussian War, 1870–1871—Juvenile fiction. [1. Gambetta,
Léon, 1838–1882—Fiction.   2. Franco–Prussian War, 1870–1871—
Fiction.   3. Balloon ascensions—Fiction.]   I. Curlee, Lynn, ill.

II. Title.

PZ7.H2688Ho   1993   92-29869

[E]—dc20   CIP

                                          AC

To John, Riva and Ariel

—D. H.

To J. D. M.

—L. C.

ORE THAN A HUNDRED YEARS AGO, during a war,

Prussian troops marched into France.

Over the countryside, through fields of grass,

through fields of mud, horses pulling cannons,

soldiers lifting their black boots, they fought their way forward.

When they reached Paris, they surrounded it in a ring.
All over France, people hung their heads.
Their leaders were trapped in Paris,
trapped inside the Prussian ring.

In Paris, the leaders talked and argued.
What could be done?
If only someone could get through the ring
and ride into the country.
If only someone could lead the people.

Shells exploded in the streets of Paris.

Men and women ran; horses reared.

There were too many Prussian soldiers with too many guns.

Who could get through?

Maybe not through, said a young man.

But over.

How can this be done? asked the leaders.

En ballon, messieurs, he said.

The young man's name was Léon Gambetta.
He would rise over the Prussian troops
and raise an army in the country
south of Paris, south of the enemy ring.

For two days fog covered Paris.
On the third day it lifted.
Léon Gambetta rose in his balloon.

The sounds of war were all around him.

A bullet grazed his hand.

But his heart was filled with the thought of saving his country.

He flew up and up, into the clouds.

It was quiet now.
And in the quiet he looked around
and saw the shapes of clouds, changing in the wind.
He wondered where he was going—
if the wind was blowing him south.

But mostly he watched the shapes . . .

shapes he'd seen as a little boy
lying in a field staring up at the sky—

a wide white sea,
horses with wings.

He looked down.

He couldn't see the land.

He couldn't hear the war.

He looked again at the clouds as he floated in silence.

The balloon seemed to hang forever.

He wanted to stay there forever.

With a start he remembered the battle below.

He remembered the enemy ring.

He stared at the clouds,

and the horses with wings stared back at him.

Slowly he descended.
The clouds opened to let him through
and sealed closed above him.
The clouds seemed to be just clouds again.

Now he could hear the far-off sounds of battle.
He knew when this war was over, there would be another.
He dropped through the sky,
and his eyes watered in the wind.

He landed in a ring of trees not far from Amiens.

He carried out the plan he had made.

Days and weeks went by,

and Léon Gambetta raised an army. . . .

Over the countryside, through fields of grass,
through fields of mud, horses pulling cannons,
soldiers lifting their black boots,
Léon Gambetta and his army fought their way toward Paris.

Léon Gambetta did not fly again.

He signed orders and made speeches.

His balloon was packed and put on a railway train.

He could hardly remember what he had seen on his flight.

But sometimes in the night—

while battles raged, while armies charged

and men and horses fell—

Léon Gambetta had dreams . . .

and once again he was floating

in a wide white sea—

in a sky full of horses with wings.